Avocado the Turtle

The One & Only

Story by

Kiara Shankar
Vinay Shankar

Illustrated by

Avantika Mishra

Library of Congress Control Number: 2020924349
ISBN:
978-1-950263-33-2 (eBook)
978-1-950263-34-9 (Paperback)
978-1-950263-35-6 (Hardcover)

First Edition: Dec 2020. Published by VIKI Publishing®, San Francisco, California, USA.

Story by Kiara Shankar & Vinay Shankar.

Illustrated by Avantika Mishra.

Avocado the Turtle wasn't a normal turtle.

Avocado was completely different.
The other turtles told her that she was
a "bad example" of the turtle community.

No other turtle was ever named after food.
They had names like Francesca and Terry.
But Avocado wasn't like them.

Turtles never came out of their shells,
but Avocado did.
She never seemed to like being inside hers.

Turtles were quiet
and did not like talking to each other,
but Avocado was different.
She always tried to have a conversation.

Avocado tried to change herself,
but it was impossible.
Nobody talked to her or played with her
because she was different.
It made Avocado feel very left out.

Everything changed one day
when the turtles decided it was time
to get rid of her.
They made her leave their territory
and told her never to come back.

Avocado felt hurt and cried.
She had no home and nobody to talk to.
She was all alone.
For the first time, she pulled herself into
her shell and didn't come out
 for a long time—until she heard
someone and felt them knocking on her shell.

"Hello? Hello?"

a friendly voice said.

Avocado came out and saw a giraffe.
She didn't say anything,
remembering what turtles were supposed to do.

"Why are you not talking?"
the giraffe asked.

Avocado tried to be silent,
but she couldn't. It was the first time
someone wanted to talk to her.

Avocado told the giraffe all about
the turtles and the rules.
She told him how she was no longer welcome.
The giraffe listened and didn't walk away
from her like turtles did.

"I'm so sorry about that.
It wasn't very nice of the turtles to
make fun of you or to send you away.
I'm glad you're here because
you shouldn't need to change yourself
for someone to like you.
You need to be yourself,"
the giraffe said, giving Avocado a hug.
"By the way, my name is Lemonade,
but you can call me Lemon.
I would love to be your friend
because you are fun to talk to.
Those turtles shouldn't be bullying you."

Avocado wasn't sure that
she was fun to talk to,
but she wanted to be Lemon's friend.
Lemon showed her around and
introduced her to his friends,
Bacon the Pig and Honey the Bee.

Avocado was scared that
they would be like the turtles,
but they turned out to be very nice
and wanted to talk to her, too.

They all spent the day playing
hide-and-seek and had a great time.
Avocado felt happy 😊
for the first time in her life.

Lemon, Bacon, and Honey were just like her
and loved doing the same things she did.
Avocado wondered if what
Lemon said was really true: that
she had been with the wrong group.

The turtles weren't very kind
and made her feel left out.
But with Lemon, Bacon, and Honey,
she felt happy and didn't want
to be with the turtles anymore.

Avocado realized Lemon was right.
She was having a fun time,
but she felt sad with the turtles.

The turtles had different ways,
but that was how they were.

It's okay to be named after food.
It's okay to be out of your shell.
It's okay to be loud.
It's okay to be who you are and be yourself.
It's what makes Avocado the one and only.

*Be yourself and embrace the moment,
even if others rejected you.*

- Avocado the Turtle

About the Authors

Kiara Shankar is a talented thirteen-year-old author/songwriter from San Francisco, California, USA. Apart from writing books and songs, she loves reading and artwork. Her debut book, *Primrose's Curse*, has been published in twelve different languages including English, Spanish, Chinese, Hindi, and more.

Vinay Shankar is Kiara's dad, a software professional who found himself inspired by his daughter's idea of writing books and songs and who decided to co-write them with her. The duo's collaborative effort is helping to bring great ideas to life!

The pop hits penned by the father-daughter duo—sung by singers Primrose Fernetise, Francesca Shankar, Marla Malvins, and SpotZ the Frenchie—are now streaming on Spotify, Apple Music, YouTube Music, Amazon Music, Deezer, and more digital music streaming platforms.

Learn more at publisher's website: **www.vikipublishing.com**

VIKI Publishing®

A place where ideas become reality!

Books | Music | Games | Branded Merchandise

Coming Soon

⚠ For Intelligent Kids Only

Kiara Shankar
Vinay Shankar

Learn more at: www.vikipublishing.com

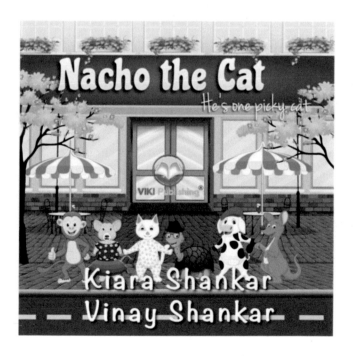